Neana
and her
Magical Adventures
1st Series

www.idapearson.com
ida.pearson@btinternet.com

Neana
and her
Magical Adventures
1st Series

Ida Pearson

First published in Great Britain in 2003
Second printing 2004
Third printing 2007

Fourth printing 2015
Published
by
Abison Publishers
Boston
Lincolnshire

A catalogue record for this book is available from the British Library.

ISBN 978-0-9555435-3-1

Contents

Neana and her Magic Garden

As Neana looked out of the window, pressing her nose against the pane of glass, she could see the raindrops glistening on the blades of grass on the large lawn belonging to the house where she lived with her Mummy and her Daddy. It had been raining all day and Neana so much wanted to go outside and play, now that it was almost summer.

The day before her Daddy had come home from work bringing Neana a kitten. He had brought it from work. He had brought it from Neana's Grandmother's home.

When Neana went to visit her Grandmother (whom she called Nan-Nan) and Grandfather (whom she called Granddad) she loved to play with Smokey the cat.

One day, her Nan-Nan told Neana that Smokey was going to have kittens, and after they were born, if Neana promised to look after a kitten by feeding and playing with it, she could have one.

After the kittens were born, Neana chose hers, and when the day finally arrived for it to be able to leave its Mummy, Neana's Daddy brought it home for Neana.

As it had been raining all day, the kitten and Neana had to play inside the big house. Although she really preferred playing in the garden, being forced to stay inside gave her time to choose a name for her new friend. Neana decided to call him Sooty as he was black all over.

'Neana,' her Mummy, called from the kitchen. Neana went running, followed by Sooty, to find her Mummy busy cooking.

'Now that the rain has stopped,' said Mummy, 'would you like to take Sooty outside for a little while before your bath?'

'Ooh yes!' Said Neana, very excited.

'You must keep to the path,' said Mummy. 'You mustn't go on the grass, as it is wet, and not into Daddy's vegetable garden either.'

Neana's Daddy had a vegetable garden, which he didn't like anyone to go into unless he was there himself. He was very particular about his garden and always liked to keep it neat and tidy with no weeds. He didn't like anyone to step onto it, making sure they kept to the path. The vegetable garden had a high fence round it and a big door leading into it.

Neana stepped outside the kitchen door onto the path, and Sooty followed. There were puddles on the path and Neana walked through them. As she only had her sandals on, the water tickled her feet. Sooty walked round the puddles, shaking his back paws when he accidentally stepped into the water.

Neana saw a large blade of grass. She pulled it out of the ground and tickled Sooty with it. He loved it and started to play.

He rolled over but, as the grass was wet, he jumped up again, leaping in the air. Neana laughed and Sooty scooted across the lawn and through a very small hole in the fence of the vegetable garden. Neana ran after him but didn't manage to catch him. She then realised that she would have to go and get Sooty out of the vegetable garden.

She hoped her Daddy wouldn't mind, if she was very careful not to step on the garden and kept to the path.

She opened the large door – she was only just tall -

enough to reach the handle. Inside the garden, she could see Sooty in the corner. Neana called his name and he went over to her. She bent down to pick him up and gently held him in her arms. As she turned to leave, she saw a bird sitting on the fence.

'Why hello,' said the bird, 'my name is Dickie Bird.'

Neana looked at the bird in surprise. Her Mummy had told her that a bird had talked to her about Neana when Neana wasn't there, but Neana didn't really believe her. But here was the bird, and it seemed that her Mummy had been telling the truth after all.

'Hello,' said Neana a little cautious.

'I'm your friend,' said Dickie Bird.

'He really *can* talk,' thought Neana.

'Would you like to follow me?' asked Dickie Bird. 'I have a surprise for you,'

Dickie Bird flew off the fence and Neana followed him, with Sooty at her heels.

It wasn't long before Dickie Bird came to a part of the garden where there was a rose bed.

"Daddy doesn't have roses in his vegetable garden," thought Neana, "how very strange."

Dickie Bird landed on a rose bush. Then, out from behind a very large, pink rose came a fairy.

'Hello Neana,' said the fairy, 'would you like to follow me and meet my friends?'

'Ooh, yes please,' said Neana in amazement, and the fairy flew over to a red rose bush, out from behind a red rose came another fairy. Next to the red rose bush was a yellow rose bush and out from behind a yellow rose came yet another fairy.

'Hello Neana,' they both said in chorus, as they danced on the petals of the roses.

The first fairy told Neana that she had a lot of surprises for her.

'My first,' she said, as she waved her magic wand, 'is this.'

Neana looked around. She couldn't believe her eyes. All around her were more pretty flowers, a blue sky and warm sunshine pouring down on them.

'Come,' said the fairy, 'follow me.'

Neana, Sooty and Dickie Bird followed the fairy, Neana giving a friendly goodbye wave to the two fairies left behind. They all followed the fairy down a long path of green grass until they came to a large glass house.

'Swish Swoo,' said the fairy, as she waved her magic wand. The glass house door slid open and inside there were lots of trees. There to meet them was a White Butterfly.

'Hello,' said the fairy, 'where is my friend Red Butterfly?'

'I will fetch her,' said the White Butterfly, as she flew away into the trees. Before long a beautiful Red Butterfly flew out of the trees towards the fairy.

'Hello,' said Red Butterfly. 'Who is this?' She fluttered her wings gently at Neana.

'This is my friend Neana,' said the fairy. 'Would you like to follow me?' And out of the glass house went the fairy, followed by Neana, Sooty, Dickie Bird and Red Butterfly. They all followed the fairy down the long green grass path until they came to a fishpond where a gnome was fishing.

'Hello,' said the fairy. 'Where is my friend?'

'I will call him,' said the gnome, and out from behind a plant pot came another gnome.

'Hello, I am Mr Gnome,' he said. 'Who is this?' He looked up at Neana.

This is my friend Neana,' said the fairy. The fairy then asked, 'Would you like to follow me?'

Neana, Sooty, Dickie Bird, Red Butterfly and Mr Gnome all followed the fairy down the long green grass path until they came to a brown gate.

'Swish Swoo,' said the fairy, as she waved her magic wand. The brown gate opened, and there, through the gate, were swings, slides, roundabouts and fair rides.

Neana and her friends swung on the swings, slid down the slides, went around on the roundabouts and rode on the fair rides.

Sooty played in the grass.

Soon it was time for a rest, after so much play.

'I'm hungry,' said Neana.

'Ok,' said the fairy, 'follow me.'

Neana, Sooty, Dickie Bird, Red Butterfly and Mr Gnome all followed the fairy down the long green grass path until they came to a green gate.

'Swish Swoo,' said the fairy, as she waved her magic wand. The green gate opened and there, through the gate, was a large field of green grass with daisies growing in it. Right in the middle was a large table and sitting around it were teddies, dollies and pandas. Right at the top of the table was a large teddy bear. The fairy went to greet him. 'Hello,' she said.

'Who is this that you have with you?' asked the large teddy bear, his big brown eyes looking lovingly at Neana.

'This is my friend Neana,' said the fairy. 'We have come to join you for tea.'

'Please sit down,' said the large teddy bear, taking hold of Neana's hand with his large paw and guiding her to a seat right next to him. 'My name is Big Ted,'

Neana's new friends followed and all sat round the large table, apart from Sooty, who sat in the grass near Neana's chair.

There was lots of different food to eat; sandwiches, jellies, ice-cream, cakes and biscuits, with orange juice to drink. Neana gave Sooty a saucer of cream. They all ate and drank as much as they could, and after tea Big Ted told them all stories, everyone sat round on the grass to listen. Neana made a daisy chain with lots of pretty pink and white daisies, while Sooty leaped about on the grass.

After the stories were finished, Neana said to the fairy, 'I'm so tired.'

'Ok,' said the fairy, 'follow me.'

Neana, Sooty Dickie Bird, Red Butterfly and Mr Gnome followed the fairy through the green gate after saying goodbye and thanking their new friends for the lovely tea. They went back onto the -

grass path, but this time it didn't seem so long and they soon came to the large garden door.

'It's time to say goodbye now,' said the fairy. 'And don't forget Neana that this is your secret magic garden! Please come again soon.'

Neana said goodbye to the fairy, Dickie Bird, Red Butterfly and Mr Gnome, thanked them for such a lovely time and promised that she would be back again very soon.

The rose bushes and all the flowers had disappeared and the sun was no longer shining as Neana walked out of the vegetable garden onto the lawn. She heard her Mummy calling. 'Time for bed Neana!'

Neana ran into the house, still feeling very excited, Sooty followed her.

Mummy had Neana's bath all ready. While she had her bath, Sooty played on the mat beside her.

Soon Neana was all ready for bed. Mummy read Neana's favourite story to her and tucked her up in bed, all warm and cosy. Then she gave Neana a goodnight kiss and a cuddle saying to her. 'Did you have fun outside with Sooty?'

'Yes,' said Neana. As she never kept secrets from her Mummy, she told her Mummy, 'I have a magic garden in Daddy's vegetable garden.'

'Do you dear? How nice,' said Mummy. 'Well, you must go to sleep now.'

Neana thought her Mummy didn't really believe her, but then she hadn't really believed her Mummy about the talking bird until she heard it for herself.

Neana turned over in her bed and reached out for her cardigan, which she had laid beside her on a stool. She put her hand into the pocket and pulled out the daisy chain and laid it gently on the stool beside her. Neana lay back on her pillow, knowing that the magic garden was real. She pulled up her bed covers and thought of her new friends. She knew she would see them again, one day very soon

Neana and her Magic Carpet

The sun was shining through the trees onto the kitchen table where Neana and her Mummy had eaten breakfast. It was a warm summer's morning.

As Neana moved away from the breakfast table her Mummy turned to her and said. 'I think today, Neana, I will sort out the loft as it is a nice sunny morning.'

'What a good idea,' said Neana. 'Can I help?'

'Well, when I've got the things down out of the loft *then* you can,' said Mummy.' It's best that you go and play while I'm doing that job, as it isn't really safe for you to be around in case I drop something.'

'Okay,' said Neana, opening the back door to let in Sooty. 'Did you have a nice walk Sooty, while Mummy and I had our breakfast?'

Sooty gave a 'meow' almost as if he knew what Neana had said. He rubbed his fur coat all around Neana's legs with his long tail straight up and a little curl at the end.

'Come on Sooty,' said Neana, 'let's play outside.'

Mummy washed up all the pots while Sooty and Neana played. Afterwards she began clearing out the loft. She laid most of the things outside on the lawn and Neana helped to carry them out.

The morning went by quickly, because there was so much to do and, before long, it was time for lunch.

After lunch Mummy decided that she would start sorting things out. Neana helped by bringing some of the things back into the kitchen ready for Mummy to find a place for them. As mummy was passing things to Neana, Neana noticed a large piece of red and grey carpet that was all rolled up. 'What a pretty carpet,' said Neana.

'I know,' said Mummy, and she started to unroll the carpet. 'You can play on it while I sort out the things in the kitchen.'

Neana couldn't wait to play on the beautiful carpet.

I will fetch you a drink,' said Mummy, 'you can sit on the carpet while you take your drink.'

Mummy went into the house to make the drink.

It wasn't long before she was walking back across the lawn, with a drink in one hand for Neana and a saucer of milk in the other hand for Sooty.

'There you are,' said Mummy. 'Now I'll get on with the sorting out in the kitchen.'

'Okay,' said Neana, making herself comfortable on the carpet, with Sooty by her side.

As she was taking her drink she saw Dickie Bird on the fence. 'Hello Neana,' said Dickie Bird, and before she could answer she saw the fairy flying down from over the fence towards her. 'Hello Neana,' said the fairy, landing close to Sooty and almost knocking over the saucer of milk. 'Did you know that this is a magic carpet?'

'Really?' said Neana. 'How?'

'I will show you,' said the fairy. 'Hold on tight!'

And the fairy waved her magic wand and said the magic words, 'Up, Up and Away!'

The carpet lifted off the ground and up over Daddy's garden fence.

'First we will pick up the rest of our friends,' said the fairy. '*Then,* I have some surprises for you,'

So, on the carpet flying high went the fairy, Neana, Sooty and Dickie Bird. Before long they came to the glass house to pick up Red Butterfly. As the glass house door opened, after the fairy had used her magic words, Swish Swoo,' and waved her magic wand, Red Butterfly fluttered her wings, came out of the glass house and landed on the carpet. 'Hello,' said Red Butterfly, 'where are we going?'

'You'll see,' said the fairy.

Next, the carpet landed near the fishpond and Mr Gnome climbed aboard.

'Up, Up and Away!' said the fairy, waving her magic wand and the carpet lifted off the ground.

'How exciting!' said Mr Gnome.

'Isn't it!' Said Neana, and they flew into the clouds which were all soft, fluffy and white.

After a while the fairy told Neana to look down and, there, below her, she saw a blue sea, sand and children playing.

'We will land here,' said the fairy. 'We can all make sandcastles.'

The carpet landed on the sand. Neana couldn't wait to get off, and she quickly took off her socks and shoes, as she loved to feel the sand tickle her toes.

They all followed the fairy and soon they were all busy making sandcastles. The children who were already on the sand all joined in and between them they made a *very* large sandcastle. Neana noticed a flag lying in the sand. She picked it up and placed it right on the very top of the sandcastle.

'That looks very nice,' said the fairy. 'As you have all worked so very hard I think it's time to go and get an ice-cream.'

So, they all followed the fairy and while they ate their ice-creams they went for a ride in a horse and carriage and loved every minute. Then, after their ride, they went back onto the sand, where Neana noticed some donkeys waiting to give the children rides. 'Please can I have a donkey ride?' she asked.

'Of course,' said the fairy.

Neana chose one of the donkeys for her ride. Its name was Molly, and Neana gave her a stroke and a friendly cuddle.

All her friends watched as she took her ride. The bells on the donkeys jingled and the children's laughter filled the air as the donkeys trotted along the sands.

On Neana's return the fairy said. 'We must all get back onto the carpet because the tide will soon be in.'

So Neana, Sooty, Dickie Bird, Red Butterfly and Mr Gnome all climbed aboard the magic carpet. The fairy waved her magic wand. 'Up, Up and Away!' -

she cried.

And the carpet flew up into the soft fluffy, white clouds.

Neana looked down at the sandcastle, just in time to see it disappearing under a large white wave. The sea was washing it away. All that was left to see was the flag, floating on top of the sea and being knocked about by the heavy waves. Neana felt sad that the sand castle had gone.

'Never mind,' said the fairy. 'Your friends on the sand will build a new one tomorrow.'

Neana then saw all her new friends eating their ice-creams in the warm sunshine on the green grass. They all waved goodbye to Neana and Neana waved back.

Before long Neana noticed another castle. 'Where are we now? She asked.

'You'll see,' said the fairy, as the carpet landed near the steps leading up to a castle.
There to meet them was the Queen of the fairies. She gave Neana a bright smile and Neana soon forgot about the disappearing sandcastle.

The Queen of the fairies held out her tiny hand to Neana and led her up the steps, through the large doors, with all of her friends following and, there to see, all was wonderment. She now realised that she was in fairy land.

There was so much to see and do. The Queen of the fairies led Neana and her friends all of the way round.

Everything surrounding Neana was so tiny; not at

all what Neana had expected to see when she first arrived at the castle steps.

The Queen of the fairies pointed across the room and Neana's eyes opened in amazement as her gaze fell on the fairy ring.

The fairies in the ring were dressed in bright and pastel colours, and in the centre was a fountain of water that showered sparkling colours from the lights above it. Neana found it hard to take her gaze away but with so much to see there was little time to stand and stare and with only a very short stay it wasn't long before it was time to leave.

Just as Neana was being led down the stone steps onto the carpet a fairy landed right beside Neana.

'Oh,' said the Queen of the fairies, 'I'm so pleased that you have arrived as you are just in time to say goodbye to Neana.'

I am so pleased to see you again,' said the fairy, 'I almost didn't make it.' Neana looked on in surprise: who can this fairy be? She thought. Her thoughts were broken into when the fairy announced to Neana. 'I am your Tooth Fairy and I will be visiting you again soon.' She fluttered her wings and flew through the castle doors, saying her goodbyes as she disappeared into the castle.

'Come,' said the fairy to Neana and her friends, 'it is time for us to climb aboard the magic carpet.'

Neana was so excited at meeting the Tooth Fairy. She continued her way up to the magic carpet followed by Sooty, Dickie Bird, Red Butterfly and Mr Gnome.

They all climbed aboard the magic carpet. The fairy waved her magic wand and said the magic words. 'Up, Up and Away,' and the carpet flew up into the soft, fluffy white, clouds again.

Neana looked down feeling happy with her visit and waved to the friends that she was leaving behind.

Before long they reached a palace.

'Here we are,' said the fairy. 'We just have time to visit here - as we are expected.'

Neana couldn't believe her eyes. There in front of her was a huge palace with large stone steps leading up to the main door.

The carpet landed, and they all climbed off onto the

first stone step to make their climb to the front door. The door opened, and there to greet them was a footman.

'Follow me,' the footman said, and he led them down a long hallway to a staircase carpeted in red, with white banisters.

'There you are,' said the footman. 'Go up to the top of the staircase to the first door.'

They all climbed the staircase and when they had reached the top, the fairy waved her magic wand and said the magic words, 'Swish Swoo,' and the door opened.

There in front of them was a large glass cabinet and inside were all the crown jewels.

The fairy waved her magic wand and said the magic words 'Swish Swoo,'

The door of the cabinet opened.

The fairy reached out for the crown, which was rather heavy and placed it on Neana's head. Neana looked at herself in the nearby mirror; the jewels in the crown sparked and glistened.

'Oh!' said Neana, 'this is so pretty!'

And she lifted the crown gently off her head and put it on the table.

The fairy then gave her a necklace, which she placed round Neana's neck. Neana touched it gently, the jewels all sparkling, but to Neana's surprise the necklace broke and all the beads rolled onto the floor. Neana was so upset.

'Don't worry,' said the fairy, and she waved her magic wand, and the necklace became all strung up again. 'Come,' said the fairy, 'we must put them all away as it is time to leave,'

They placed the jewels back into the cabinet.

The fairy waved her magic wand, and the door closed.

Then they made their way back onto the landing. Neana turned to have one last look at the jewels and as she did so she noticed a bead shining in the corner, on the floor. Neana walked across the room and picked up the bead, then walked to the fairy and placed the bead in her hand, the fairy said. 'You can keep the bead, as my gift to you.'

'Oh, thank you!' said Neana, and she placed the bead gently in her pocket.

'Come,' said the fairy, 'we must hurry now.'

They all walked along the landing, past a balcony. Neana glanced down and saw all the kings, queens, princes and princesses of the land in their tuxedos, ball gowns and fine jewellery.

'Come,' said the fairy, 'time for us to go home.'

Neana glanced down one more time and noticed a princess very much like herself. She looked up at Neana and gave Neana a friendly smile and a wave. Neana waved and smiled back. She paused as she did so, and then continued to follow the fairy and the rest of her friends.

Neana, Sooty, Dickie Bird, Red Butterfly and Mr Gnome boarded the magic carpet.

'Up, Up and Away!' said the fairy, as she waved her magic wand, and again the carpet flew up into the soft, fluffy, white clouds. Neana looked down at the palace, thinking of the little princess and wishing that she too could be a princess but feeling excited with the thoughts of her visit

Before long the carpet landed on Neana's lawn.

'We must go now,' said the fairy, it's time for your bed.'

Neana said goodbye to all of her friends and promised that she would see them again soon.

As Neana and Sooty stepped off the carpet, Mummy called to Neana. 'Time for bed Neana dear.'

Neana ran into the house with Sooty in her arm.

After such an exciting day, Neana was very tired and it wasn't long before she was all ready for bed and Mummy was tucking her in and giving her a goodnight kiss and cuddle. Sooty was already fast -

asleep.

'Go to sleep now,' said Mummy.

'I will,' said Neana. 'But before I do, I have to tell you that the carpet on the lawn is a magic one.'

She told Mummy all about her day, and how she wished that she too was a princess. Mummy sat beside Neana on her bed and held her hand.

When Neana had finished talking, Mummy said. 'But you *are* a princess, you are mine and Daddy's princess, and you always will be.' She gave Neana a gentle kiss and pulled up her covers. Time for sleep,' Mummy whispered and went quietly out of the room.

Neana reached out her hand to pick up her cardigan, which she had placed on the stool beside her bed. She felt into her pocket and pulled out the bead. She placed it gently on the stool and lay back on her pillow, happy knowing that she too was a princess.

Neana and her Magic Box

It was Saturday morning, and, although it wasn't yet quite winter, with the cold weather it seemed like it.

Neana awoke feeling rather sad, as her Daddy had gone away on business for the weekend. Usually on a weekend all the family would go on an outing. Sometimes they would travel a long distance and sometimes only a short one, but it made no difference to Neana where she went, as she really loved to go out. This week wouldn't be the same without Daddy.

'Oh,' thought Neana sadly, and she turned over and pulled her covers over her shoulders and snuggled back down, only to hear her Mummy calling. 'Neana! Time to get up, your breakfast is ready!'

Neana threw back her covers and climbed out of bed unwillingly. She put on her slippers and dressing gown and combed her hair. Then she made her way towards the kitchen. Mummy was already sitting at the table drinking her cup of tea. She placed the cup down on the saucer and smiled at Neana 'Good morning Neana,' she said.

Neana smiled back. Seeing the smile on her Mummy's face made her feel a little better, although she still felt a bit sad.

'I wish Daddy was here,' said Neana.

'I know dear,' said Mummy. 'But he will soon be home again.

'But I like it when we all go out together at the weekend,' said Neana.

'Well, maybe we still can,' said Mummy. 'You and I will go somewhere,'

'But it's not the same without Daddy,' said Neana.

Mummy gave Neana one of her special smiles and pulled out her chair. 'Sit down dear, eat your breakfast – it won't be as bad as you think,' she said placing her hand on Neana's shoulder and giving her a gentle, loving squeeze.

Neana was about to take a drink out of her cup when the telephone rang.

'There,' said Mummy. 'That might be Daddy now would you like to answer the telephone?'

'Yes please!' said Neana and raced to pick up the telephone.

It was Nan-Nan. Neana felt excited at hearing her voice. After a little chat with Neana, Nan-Nan asked to speak to Mummy. 'I may have a little surprise for you, if Mummy agrees,' she said.

Neana called her Mummy to the telephone. As Mummy took the telephone from Neana, Neana clasped her Mummy's hand excitedly, pulling at it saying, 'Nan-Nan has a surprise for me!'

'Shush,' said Mummy, trying hard to listen to what Nan-Nan was saying above Neana's noisy excitement. Then she said, 'I'm sure that will be all right. We'll see you in a little while.'

She placed the telephone back on its cradle.

'*Please* tell me, Mummy!' said Neana excitedly.

'Sit down and eat your breakfast, and I will tell you,' said Mummy. 'Nan-Nan and Granddad are coming over to take us out in their car. We haven't long to get ready, as they will be here in a little while, so we must be quick.'

Mummy let Sooty in after his morning walk.

'Hello Sooty,' said Neana, 'we're going out with Nan-Nan and Granddad today.'

Sooty gave a 'meow' as Neana bent down to stroke his soft fur.

'We won't be able to take Sooty,' said Mummy. 'He can stay in his basket with his toys,'

Neana walked up the stairs to her bedroom to get ready, while Mummy tidied up the kitchen. Neana quickly dressed and tidied up her bedroom. She heard a car pull into the drive. "That must be Nan-Nan and Granddad," she thought, and quickly went down the stairs and raced to open the front door.

Nan-Nan and Granddad were just stepping out of the car. 'Hello Neana,' they both chorused. 'How are you today?' Granddad asked Neana.

Neana ran to them both and gave them a big hug.

As they walked into the house, Neana heard her Mummy calling, 'put on your coat! It's *very* cold today, so you will also need your hat, gloves, scarf and boots.'

So Neana wrapped herself up warm.

'Are we ready now?' Nan-Nan asked.

'Yes,' said Mummy, placing a saucer of milk on the floor for Sooty.

Neana gave her kitten a cuddle and put him gently in his basket.

They all walked out of the house and climbed into the car.

'Where shall we go?' asked Granddad.

'I know,' said Neana, 'on the swings and slides.'

'Okay,' said Granddad.

Before long they arrived at the park.

There weren't many children there and it wasn't long before Neana found out why. Her Mummy was right – it was a *very* cold day, and Neana's hands and feet soon became very cold.

'I'm *so* cold,' said Neana.

'Yes, I think we shall have to go,' said Mummy.

Neana climbed back into the car, feeling rather miserable.

'I know, let's go for a nice warm drink,' said Nan-Nan.

They made their way to a restaurant, which was just like the park – almost empty.

Neana wasn't very hungry or thirsty and continued to feel rather miserable. However, Granddad persuaded Neana to have a hot chocolate drink and a cream biscuit. 'It might make you feel better,' he said.

So, they all sat round the table in the restaurant, and although it was nice and warm and the hot chocolate drink and cream biscuit were nice, Neana still felt a little miserable. Mummy, Nan-Nan and Granddad chatted away to each other and seemed -

happy, but Neana sat quietly, thinking of what she could do for the rest of the day.

After a short while they all left the warm restaurant and went back to the car, only to find, as they stepped outside, that it was pouring with rain.

'Oh no!' said Neana.

'Yes, it is awful weather isn't it?' said Nan-Nan, and they all hurried to the car.

'I know, we can go to the antique shop,' said Nan-Nan. 'I haven't been there for quite a while and the man who owns the shop is so nice.'

'That's a good idea,' said Mummy.

Neana thought that it wasn't a good idea at all, but as there wasn't anywhere else to go she had no choice.

Granddad soon stopped the car near the antique shop, and the man who owned the shop came out to greet them. 'You can park your car there, right by the shop,' he said to Granddad. He did so, and they all climbed out of the car.

'Hello,' said the shop man to Neana, putting his hand in his pocket and bringing out a bag of sweets, 'Would you like a sweet?'

'Ooh, yes please,' said Neana. "Nan-Nan was right he *is* a nice man," she thought.

The shop owner held out the bag to the others, then opened the door and led the way inside his shop. As Neana walked in she noticed that, although it was warm in the shop, it did seem a bit dark and dismal.

Nan-Nan, Mummy and Granddad started to look

around. Neana looked to see what was on the shelves but as they were high, she couldn't see some of the things.

Now Neana was feeling *really* miserable and wished that she was at home with Sooty. She started to walk through the shop, looking at some of the objects on the shelves but not being really interested, that is, until she saw a bright shiny box, which seemed to have all the colours of the rainbow on it. Somehow it seemed to brighten the place up. Neana was about to pick it up when she heard her Mummy's voice. 'Don't touch, Neana dear,'

Neana pulled back her hands and the owner came over to her. 'Do you like the box?' he asked.

'I would like to have a look at it,' said Neana.

'I know,' said the man, 'would you like to look round my toy department?'

'Yes please,' replied Neana.

'I'll ask my assistant to open the door for you, and if your Mummy agrees, you can take a look.

Mummy nodded her head and a smile came to Neana's face.

'While my assistant opens the door, you can take a look at the box,' said the owner.

Neana walked back to where the box was on the shelf. She gazed up and down the shelf and noticed a birdcage, and right on the top of the cage was Dickie Bird. He flew down and landed on the box. 'Hello Neana,' he said. 'Please open the box, there's a surprise in there for you.'

Neana gently opened the lid of the box and there inside, just waking up, rubbing her eyes was the fairy. 'Hello Neana!' I've been waiting for you,' she said. As the fairy climbed out, Neana noticed that the inside of the box was all lined with red velvet. Then she heard the owner's voice. 'You can go through to my toy department now Neana.'

She looked down the shop and saw an open door at the far end.

'We'll wait here for you,' said Mummy.

'Okay,' said Neana.

The fairy then told Neana that she would see her in the toy department, and off she flew, with Dickie Bird.

Neana couldn't get to the door quickly enough, she was so excited. As she walked through the doorway, she gazed round at all the shelves that were piled high with toys. Fairy lights along the shelves made the department look bright and cheerful.

Neana looked up to the very top of the shelves and noticed some toy butterflies, hanging from pieces of string, and swirling round in the cool breeze that was coming in through the small open window. Just as Neana was about to look away, one of the butterflies left its string, flew down and landed on a miniature village. Neana walked across to it.

'Hello Neana,' said Red Butterfly, and there in the miniature garden, were the fairy and Dickie Bird.

'We have two of us missing,' said Red Butterfly.

'No, we don't,' said a voice behind a small miniature pot, and out popped Mr Gnome.

'Sooty couldn't come,' said Neana.

'I will sort that out for you,' said the fairy. She waved her magic wand and, when Neana looked down, there was Sooty at her feet.

'I have some surprises for you Neana. 'Follow me,' said the fairy.

Neana, Sooty, Dickie Bird, Red Butterfly and Mr Gnome all followed the fairy until they came to a large doll's house.

Swish Swoo,' said the fairy, waving her magic wand, and the door of the doll's house opened and they all walked inside.

There were *so* many toys to see. Toy soldiers stood in a neat line with their musical instruments by their sides. There was a large doll in the corner with long dark hair and a ribbon placed round her head, wearing a dress made of silk to match her pink ribbon and white shiny shoes. Big Ted sat in an armchair with his big brown eyes shining. A panda lay on his bed on top of his covers, and there was a ballerina doll lying on the floor.

'This is your surprise,' said the fairy. She waved her magic wand and said the magic words. 'Beedar Beedoo.'

And before there very eyes, all the toys came alive! The toy soldiers played their musical instruments and the large doll came over to Neana and asked her to dance. 'Isn't this fun,' said the doll to Neana.

'Ooh, yes,' said Neana, as they danced together.

Big Ted came over to Neana. 'I know you, you came to my tea party!' he said.

The panda climbed out of his bed and joined the others to have a dance. The ballerina leapt off the floor, high on her toes, and twirled round to the music. They all danced and danced until the fairy asked if they would like to go on a train ride.

'Ooh, yes please!' Replied Neana.

'Follow me,' said the fairy, and Neana Sooty, Dickie Bird, Red Butterfly and Mr Gnome, with all the toys from the doll's house, followed the fairy to a train set. The fairy told them all to climb aboard.

The fairy waved her magic wand and said the magic words. 'Beedar Beedoo.'

And the train went around the track, through the tunnel and over the hills.

'Ooh, that tickles my tummy,' said Neana as the train went over a hill. They all laughed and had so much fun. But all too soon it came to an end.

The fairy stopped the train and said that they all must leave, as it was time to go. The toys went back into the doll's house and back to their places, staying still and quiet. Dickie Bird, Red Butterfly and Mr Gnome said goodbye to Neana.

'I will see you again soon,' Neana said.

The fairy then waved her magic wand and Sooty disappeared back into his basket at home.

'You must also go now,' said the fairy to Neana. 'But first, the box which you saw in the other part of the shop is not only a treasure chest but also a magic box, and you are allowed three wishes at any one time.'

'Really!' said Neana.

'But I must go now,' said the fairy, and she said goodbye to Neana. Neana promised that she would see her again soon.

Neana made her way to the door leading to the other part of the shop, turning to wave goodbye to all her friends. Then she stepped out of the toy department to be greeted by the shop owner, holding in his hands the magic box.

'Have you had a nice time Neana?' As it is a magic box, I will give it to you as a present,' said the shop owner, '

'Thank you,' said Neana.

The owner wrapped the box up in white tissue paper and placed it in a bag. '*Do* be careful with it,' he said as he handed the box to Neana.

'I will,' said Neana, and thanked him again.

Granddad held open the shop door, and Neana stepped outside to find it had stopped raining and the sun was shining.

'Did you have a nice time Neana?' Nan-Nan asked

'Ooh, yes,' said Neana, as she climbed into the car. She started to tell them of her adventure, placing the box gently on her knee and holding it tightly.

'You are right Nan-Nan,' Neana said, 'that shop owner *is* nice, and he gave me this magic box.'

They decided to spend the rest of the day at Nan-Nan and Granddad's house. Nan-Nan put the box in a safe place until it was time for Neana to leave. Neana played with Smokey, as she knew Sooty would be far too tired to play after his adventure at the toy department with Neana and the rest of her friends.

After they had had tea, Granddad got the car out of the garage to drive Neana and Mummy home.

Neana said goodbye to Nan-Nan and thanked her for taking her out, as it was a good idea after all to go to the antique shop. Nan-Nan handed Neana the box.

Neana and Mummy climbed into the car and they set off down the road, Neana waved to her Nan-Nan until she disappeared into the distance.

They arrived home soon afterwards. Sooty was fast asleep in his basket and Neana got ready for bed.

Mummy came to say goodnight. 'Daddy will be home tomorrow,' she said.

'I have *so* much to tell him,' said Neana, as Mummy gave her a kiss and cuddle.

Neana leaned over her bed to reach out for her magic box, which she had placed on the stool beside her. She opened it and placed the daisy chain and bead inside.

Then she closed the lid gently, thinking to herself that she would only use the wishes when she really needed them, and would save them until she did.

Then Neana lay back on her pillow, realising that the day had been all right after all and in future it would be okay for Daddy to go away, and that Mummy had told her lots of times that Nan-Nan was usually right. But this time, not only Nan-Nan but also Mummy had been right, and she decided that she would always try to remember this in the future.

Neana fell fast asleep happy with the thoughts of seeing her Daddy the next day.